Berit Ellingsen

Vessel and Solsvart

THIS IS A SNUGGLY BOOK

ISBN: 978-1-943813-26-1

Acknowledgements: 'Vessel and Solsvart' was first published in *Birkensnake no. 6*, 2013; 'Among the Living and the Dead' was first published in *New Dead Families*, 2013; 'Apotheosis' was first published in *Psycho Holosuite*, 2015; 'Blue Star, Singular Fire' was first published in *Gone Lawn*, 2013; 'Summer Dusk, Winter Moon' was first published in *Transactions of the Flesh: A Homage to Joris-Karl Huysmans* (Zagava and Ex Occidente Press, 2013)

Berit Ellingsen

Vessel and Solsvart

Berit Ellingsen is the author of two novels, *Not Dark Yet* (Two Dollar Radio, 2015), and *Une ville vide* (PublieMonde, 2013), as well as a collection of short stories, *Beneath the Liquid Skin* (Queen's Ferry Press, 2012). Her work has been published in W.W. Norton's *Flash Fiction International*, *SmokeLong Quarterly*, *Unstuck*, *Litro*, and other places, and has been nominated for the Pushcart Prize, Best of the Net, and the British Science Fiction Association Award. She travels between Norway and Svalbard in the Arctic, and is a member of the Norwegian Authors' Union.

Contents

Vessel and Solsvart

Vessel and Solsvart

THE new heat reaches us from the seeping marsh, the lichen-veiled trees, and our soft bedding of moist sphagnum moss. The water, which used to be as cool as a mallard's feet, is now as warm as bat blood, the trunks that were hunched and slowly being choked by vines stretch like flowers in the sun, and the glistening purple earthworms that used to peek up through the moss are no longer here.

Vessel sits up. His eyes are milky, with a stripe of black cutting across the eyeball, deltas of red at the edges.

His lips are gone, exposing his teeth, they are still quite white. Tiny beads cover his brow and the bridge of what's left of his nose, like the droplets that seep out when you cut a fruit in half. He wipes the moisture away with a worm-eaten hand, then smiles at me, the missing lips making him look genuinely happy.

"It's turning warmer," Vessel says, his voice like dry leaves. "Like last time?"

"The sun is coming back," I say. "We must prevent it."

"It's been cloudy for as long as I can recall," he says and strokes my back with one fleshless digit.

"You don't remember how it used to be."

He drags himself to the edge of our mound, a crocodile nest hidden in the swamp grass, then leans forward and splashes brown water across his face and neck. He pulls his t-shirt off, it's just a few strings of once-white cotton looping around his chest and shoulders, but he keeps it nevertheless. He dips the remnants of the garment in the water, kneads a few times, then folds it up and wrings it, slaps the moist fabric out and pulls it back on, now patterned with rotten grass and other detritus. His black pants had two pockets down either leg, but now only the upper left pouch is still there.

I used to mock him, but then he found a soft crocodile nest in the middle of the marsh and rolled and rolled and rolled with the poor crocodile mother and her three toothy children until the water frothed red and sloshed far up on the muddy bank, and the reptiles left while they hissed loudly at us, and I took care of the eggs.

"I'll call you Solsvart," he said. "That means Blackbird."

He sits down, stretches his legs out in front of him and ties two moss-furred branches, one along the outside of his right thigh and the other along the inner thigh, with thick-barked ivy vines in looping, tight knots. When he is finished, he pushes himself up and hobbles, leg out, down to the rowboat on the bank.

The old craft is even more diminished than last time we were awake. Beetles and maggots have eaten away at the rim, the wood is as smooth and gray as the tree trunks that float ashore at the coast. The previously broad blade of the single oar that is left is now barely wider than the shaft. But the bottom of the boat is still intact, covered by orange and brown and yellow leaves.

I hop up on the bow and he leans onto the stern and pushes the rowboat out into the languid current. LGreen water lily stems waft like tendrils in the wake of the ancient wood, which causes a fragrance of decay to rise from the water. The boat scrapes along the mud, then floats. Vessel throws himself on the transom, pulls himself forward and slides down on the leaves. They crinkle in protest and two gray centipedes scuttle up from the dryness and over the rim.

We move slowly through the night, the cloud cover like a lid, as it has been for almost as long as I can remember. Across the still surface a loon calls for her lover. Frogs and cicadas fill the air with noise. Bats, their silhouettes darker than the gloom, cut the fetid air with their wings. A moth the size of Vessel's head flutters out of the blackness, a pale blotch shaped like a human skull flashing on its back. Vessel shouts and ducks and ruffles the hair he has left.

"I hate moths," he mutters. Then he lies down again on the dry leaves and I alight on his chest.

The current takes us to a narrow but deep stream that curls through the forest. Beneath us luminescent fish glitter like gold coins. Sparse foliage covered with dust scrapes the bow and sides. I glance up now and then, but Vessel remains still. The water clucks and chortles against the worm-pitted wood.

The little stream grows larger and larger and brighter and brighter in color, until it is almost beige and so wide the wall of vegetation on both sides of it sink into the morning mist. The boat tilts with the pull of the current and increases in speed. Vessel springs up, glances around, then pulls the oar out from the bottom of the rowboat and plunges it into the churning water. A short while of furious staking brings us down across the current to the opposite shore. At the first sight of a sandy bank, Vessel steers the boat on land. There, he pulls the ancient wood up into the underbrush, then starts walking upstream along the river.

The City of Stone

After a day's journey along the riverbed, the trees thin to bushes, then give way to a grassy moor that stretches inland. We leave the water's edge and follow the heath towards the foothills in the distance. There is only the soft sound of the tip of the oar against the ground as Vessel leans onto the shaft while he makes his way across the plain, the whisper of grass against his legs, and the susurration from the insects that surround us. We continue day and night.

When the ground has turned dry and gray with pebbles and sand, the foothills come much closer. The pale outline of a path winds along the steep slopes. We follow it up into the mountains.

"Stay on the path to the next peak," I tell Vessel after a trip in the air. At the summit, which is lower than the others around us, the ground is white and very cold, like it is in the high north, but when we are across the watershed, the path turns dusty and stone-filled again.

As we start the descent, the trail sidles past a blade-edged crag, a wide plateau with geometrical shapes; rectangles and squares of all sizes, interspersed with parallel lines, and the occasional circle, more lines, and more rectangles, comes into view. It looks like a maze constructed from right angles only.

We descend the final slope and enter the City of Stone. The geometrical patterns are created by long, low walls made of enormous stone blocks. Scattered along the walls are mounds and piles of cracked mineral and broken stone. Here and there a corner is still standing—two walls leaning into one another, or a jagged piece of floor jutting out from a wall like a path to the heavens. Other places we see the zig-zag traces of staircases that once climbed the stone, or the wooden remnants of shutters and doors. It is impossible to guess how high the walls once were. Now they barely reach to Vessel's thigh, and all their edges are worn concave by the dust and wind. We enter the outlines which the un-known structures have left on the ground, but all we find are more col-lapsed walls, debris and stone. There are no other sounds than the shrieking of the wind through the broken walls and the crunch of Vessel's footsteps on the ground. The air smells of snow, yet even at this elevation there is a moist warmth to the air, like perspira-tion, and the days are brighter than in the lowland.

Occasionally, Vessel lies down on his back in the gravel. I curl up in the crook of his arm as I'm afraid the wind will pick me up and hurl me across the ground before I wake.

The City of Stone turns light and dark a few times more. In the distance, rays of sunlight break through the rushing clouds. The wind never ceases or dies down. We find a lump of more than a dozen rats stuck in a hole at the bottom of a wall. The rodents' tails have been tangled together, broken at the knots, healed crooked, and fused together, so no individual could go where it wanted to. Their skin is dry and buckled, as if it has been cured, and their little claws curl helplessly beneath their bodies. They have been dead for so long they don't even smell. We walk on.

It grows dark and light and dark again. The field of walls and mounds and gravel does not end. The wind becomes a constant whistling in our ears.

Let's go back," I say.

Vessel grins and starts walking down the remnants of a street.

"This way," I say and turn in the direction of the mountains in the distance. There, beyond rows and rows of fallen barriers, is the slope we came down from and the path that clings to its side.

"No, this is a city and we shall treat it as one," Vessel says. He follows the dead traces of streets and roads back to the foothill, even when only open stretches or completely collapsed walls separate us from our goal.

The City of Trees

We descend the mountains and the foothills, cross the heath, and return to the broad, warm river. The boat is where we left it on the taupe-colored bank.

"Let's follow the river to the ocean," I say. "Perhaps we will find what we seek there."

Vessel pushes the old wood back into the cloudy current, pulls himself up on the stern and crawls down into the leaf-covered bottom. I settle on his chest and together we travel slowly to the coast.

It is night when we arrive. There is a faint glow in the sky from the full moon, but it cannot break through the clouds. Our boat crunches ashore. The gravel beach curves gently up from the ocean, which is as black and gleaming as a crow's eye.

Vessel pushes the rowboat further up on land and with a heave and a stumble, turns the boat around. Its rounded bow and broad flanks gouge deep gashes into the sand and oily water rushes in to fill the depressions.

We begin to walk, not as close to the sea as to be slowed down by the fine, gray sand deposited there, or as far up on land as to be hindered by the tall, sharp grass growing there. Instead, we walk along the part of the shore that has been packed dense and hard by the ocean's constant heartbeat. A slow surf hisses along the beach, depositing reams of piss-yellow foam that rolls and flutters like flags in the breeze. Here and there we pass the remains of tree trunks, branches and seaweed that have been washed ashore. They are dry and smooth and have been turned to stone by time and the unending wind. We more feel than see the ocean, pushing against us in wave after wave, slowly swallowing the land.

We follow the coastline for several days and nights. None of us say any-thing, but it's an easy silence. When the shore becomes lined with low fir trees, blushing bilberry shrub and purple heather, we turn inland. The underbrush soon gives way to a carpet of yellow fir needles. Row upon row of brown trunks and green canopies stretch out in every direction and dampen the wind to a whisper. The air is heavy with the scent of tree sap and rotting wood. Only gnarled roots, jagged rocks and reddish-black anthills break the monotony of the endless ranks of trees.

"I smell smoke," Vessel says, sniffing the air. "Do you?"

I look up at the ragged patch of sky that is barely visible between the dark treetops.

"Perhaps it is from the City of Trees?" I say.

We follow the scent of the smoke. Vessel's oar-leaning footsteps make almost no sound on the thick fir needles. Soon I can smell the smoke too. Night falls, then dawn, then night again. It is warm and the silence hums in our ears.

We enter a clearing and then we see the city, above us, in the trees. Circular wooden platforms held aloft by fans of narrow struts fill the sky like clouds. We can make out the dark shapes of structures atop the platforms—small dwellings with domed roofs. Between the platforms stretch long rope bridges and garlands with hanging lanterns and rope ladders that descend nearly to the ground.

But the trees and platforms are charred black and the ground is gray with ashes that whirl up and dust the air. Most of the platforms have split and fallen down. Seared tree trunks and the remnants of rope bridges and huts stick out of the ashes. Spiraling ferns flash green among the gray. Saplings and vines stretch up, but the canopies above them have already started to retake the sky.

Vessel walks over to a piece of

rope that dangles from a platform and tugs at it. The fiber turns to dust in his hand.

"Here I can't go," he says.

"I will be back shortly," I say and fly up. Vessel sits down on a fallen trunk and leans against the fir behind it.

I check every platform and dwelling I can see, but find among the singed walls and perforated floors only the remnants of tables and stools, cracked pottery, and burned bones. As I land on the edge of a wooden disc, it creaks loudly, breaks off, plunges to the ground in a cloud of ashes, and tumbles into the ferns.

Vessel slowly stands, then limps over to inspect. The wayward structure has tipped a charred fir over, leaving a net of roots hanging like wet hair from the end of the overturned trunk. Vessel leans forward and peers into the hole. He hunches down and pulls out a bundle of blackened snakes. The serpents are coiled tightly around one another into long ropes, each as thick as Vessel's lower arms, and are as crisp and brittle as the burned wood around us.

"They were too busy mating to care about the fire," Vessel says. He tosses the cluster of seared snakes into the soot and rubs his hands on his trousers. There is nothing here for us.

We can't follow the scent back, so I fly up over the cone-shaped canopies and look for the dream-like glimmer of the sea to set us on the right course. This must be done several times a day, as Vessel has a tendency to walk in circles when he hasn't got his bearings. On the long trek back, we speak only once.

"Is that what everything will look like when the sun has eaten us?" I say.

The City of Reeds

When we are back at the hissing shore, we follow the coast north for two days and two nights. We progress fast as the gravel is easy to walk on and there is nothing to confuse our sense of direction.

On the second night we see something on the beach, partly on land, half bobbing in the waves. Tiny black flies cover the ground like billowing black lace and parts before Vessel's bare and grime-streaked feet with a sharp and angry hum. An overpowering smell of putrefaction drowns out the scent from the sea, and we are not surprised when we see that the thing in the water is the slime-covered corpse of a giant squid. The mottled, spindle-shaped form is at least four times longer than our rowboat and the two leading tentacles twice the length of the body itself. Its ten muscular limbs are as thick as tree trunks yet waft limply in the surf, tangling and sliding into one another. The bulging, gelatinous corpse has ruptured along the side and spilled its precious catch in a long reeking mound; glistening herring, slim sardines, and tiny gray shrimp, black crabs with legs the length of Vessel's arms, a couple of rusty-red octopi, and the saw-toothed jaw of a small sperm whale.

An enormous eye as wide as Vessel is tall stares out onto the beach and the rustling heath beyond. Through the transparent skin, we see that black pigment covers the back of the eyeball. In the faint light from the ocean it gleams like silver.

Vessel places his hands by the dead animal's eye, leans forward and pushes so the soft flesh quakes and quivers. He wades into the dead school of fish and crustaceans, and shoves at the middle. Then he pushes at the animal's broadest, fin-adorned end before he moves back to the head. He pushes and pulls until he manages to shift the enormous corpse enough for the waves to take hold of it and drag it out to sea with them. Gas bubbles to the surface in a torrent of sound and smell, but the squid vanishes into the depths. Afterwards Vessel scrubs his hands and feet in the black water for a long time.

※

The next morning we reach the City of Reeds. But the beach is empty, not even a twig of driftwood or a blade of seaweed can be seen on the shore. There is only sand and pebbles and Vessel's three-legged footprints unfurling in a long tail behind us.

"This is where the City of Reeds used to be," I say.

Vessel looks around. Out in the deeper water, a swell lifts and crests and is illuminated from behind by the gray dawn that shines in from the horizon. For a brief moment, dark forms and shapes appear deep inside the wave before the fluid wall crashes down and rolls unimpeded towards the shore. Vessel wrings off the tatters of his shirt, unties the thin branches that support his leg, pulls off his pants and hobbles out into the water.

"Here, I cannot follow," I say and settle on the smooth gray pebbles while the wind ruffles the feathers on my back.

Vessel limps out into the gray waves until only his head peeks above the surface and the long strands of hair that still stick to his skull float like black kelp about it. Then even they disappear into the water.

I close my eyes and imagine Vessel suspended between the dark ocean floor and the bright sea surface like a bird in a breathing sky. There, among luminescent cold-water reefs, mounds of gray brain coral, billowing black nudibranchs and blood-red sea anemones, he sees glazed roofs and hedge-bounded gardens in a grid of streets lined with vehicles and garbage bins and lamps. Some of the houses have sharply slanting roofs, horizontal siding, and small windows with sheer silk curtains that sway in the water. Other homes have flat roofs and floor-to-ceiling glass doors and white vertical blinds floating out through a gap in the transparent barrier. In the gardens Vessel spots old pear trees, cherry saplings, red rhubarb spreading its wide leaves over the lawn, maples, birches, larks, white roses, pink honeysuckle, and orange lilies. But he sees no people and no animals, only empty gardens and houses.

The day passes and darkens to night. It is noticeably warmer than before we set out on our journey. The black surf rolls lazily onto land, occasionally sending a spray of salty drops my way. I see a faint motion out among the gloomy waves, like the slick head of a seal or an otter, but it's Vessel, slowly swimming towards the shore. He continues until he's almost on land, then stands up and limps out of the surf. He wrings his hair and shakes the moisture off his hands, then puts his dry clothes back on.

"Did you find anything?" I say.

"Lots," he smiles and sea water tumbles out of his lipless mouth and down his chest. "Gardens, houses, roads, but the roads were cracked and broken, the gardens covered in weeds and the houses empty and peeling. The vehicles were rusted apart and everything was dark and quiet. I saw no one, neither living nor dead."

"I saw you among the houses and the gardens, the trees were still green and lights glowed in some of the windows," I say.

"I'm afraid it wasn't so," Vessels says.

"Did you find anything that can help us stop the sun?"

"No, not a single object, except for starfish and sea kelp and corals."

"Then we have failed in our stewardship again." I bow my neck and a cold tear forces itself out of my eye and down my beak.

Vessel folds his time-eaten hands around me, picks me up and puts me on his shoulder, which is somehow still warm.

"One more place," he says.

The City of Tar

Tar is said to have been a wealthy city once, glittering at the edge of the boiling marshes that separate the endless fir forests from the icy wastes. Others claim Tar used to be an extensive factory that squeezed bitumen from the bog, liquefied the black material and shipped it south beyond the tundra. Avenues of rusty pipes still criss-cross Tar like old scars, and rows of circular tanks gape silently into the dusk-dark sky. Tar is still gleaming, but now from a thousand flickering, dripping torches that fill the air with a greasy, black smoke that mixes with the stench of decomposition from the bog and the odor of the city's own pitch-smeared buildings. Since offal and nastier wastes are thrown right out of the sheds and shacks and into the marsh, we smell Tar long before we get there.

Despite its quivering luminance, Tar is nearly quiet. The most prominent noise is Vessel's slow steps on the petrified wooden planks that lead from the edge of the bog to the dark cluster of buildings in its middle that is Tar. Behind the sound of Vessel's walking, there is a creaking and grating and whirring. Between the pipes and tanks we see the silhouettes of tall pumps that dip their heads into the tar, again and again and again. Occasionally we hear the sound of shutters opening and closing behind us and the murmur of voices. The torches sputter and hiss and somewhere nearby water drip-drip-drips.

As we cross the street between a dark staircase and a narrow alley we see a shadow moving quickly away from us. Vessel shouts and hobbles after it. I lift and chase the shadow too. We turn corner after corner, deeper and deeper into the maze of tarred and sagging wood. A pebble flies out of the darkness towards me, like an undiscovered asteroid. I circle higher. Vessel, oar in hand, catches up to the stranger.

The person turns toward us. It is a head taller than Vessel, with skin the color of lard drawn taut over sharp bones, round blue eyes that blink out of sequence on either side of a narrow skull, a thin axe-head of a nose running down its face and a mouth that reaches almost behind its neck. Its fingers are so long they fan out on the planks, yet its feet are round like table-legs, wrapped in mud-caked rags. Between its arms hang what I at first think is a bag or a pouch, but which turns out to be a stomach flapping out of its cracked chest.

He stares at Vessel's hands, then motions for us to follow. The tar person leads us along the bitumen-dark streets to a small building with a flat roof and glass windows that are still intact. The cloudy panes glow a faint, misty blue.

"Tomorrow at dawn," the tar person smacks.

Vessel inclines his head. Our guide then takes us to a shack at the edge of the maze, up a creaking staircase that winds along a naphthalene-stinking wall to a lopsided door on the second floor. At first the door seems stuck in the frame, but our host pulls until the barrier slams open and bangs into the wall behind it. The tar person takes down the torch that hangs by the door. The cone of quivering, smoky light reveals a room about the length and width of our rowboat, with a bed on the wall furthest from the door.

The tar being puts the torch back into the holder and scuttles head first down the wall. Vessel removes the torch and puts it out by stepping on it, grinding it to ashes under his dirty, long-nailed feet. Inside, he feels the lock for a key but finds none. When he sits down on the gray wool blanket on the bed dust plumes from it. Vessel pulls his legs up, swivels around and lies down on his back. He blinks a few times, then falls silent. I settle on his chest and dream about the curtains wafting behind the windows in the City of Reeds.

I wake Vessel in the middle of the night. He groans and turns over to re-enter his rest. I bite his right earlobe, the one that has the most flesh left on it.

"Time to search," I say.

Vessel climbs up on the building and from there he crawls across the rooftops while I guide him from the air back to the structure with the glowing windows. There he creeps in through a hole in the wall.

Luminescent blue lichen fills the corners and streaks the walls and ceiling, affording just enough light to see by. Dried mud crunches underfoot. The room is empty save for a cabinet in the back. Flanking the cabinet are two dusty beeswax candles in heavy pewter holders. The candles are bent like the necks of swans searching for food beneath the marsh surface and are so long the wicks lean against the dirty floor.

Vessel slides the cabinet open, its innards glowing with fungal luminescence. On a cushion of red velvet dotted with green mold sits a skeletal right hand. Thick rings bearing smooth mineral ovals adorn the thumb, middle and little finger. Another shelf contains the bones of a child's left foot. Further down is a mounted right foot, the toenails curved and filthy. On the bottom shelf is a carving in polished granite depicting a mass of ropy limbs that curl and slither and slip into one another. The knot has no beginning and no end and makes me think of rat tails tangled so tightly that their owners can't move, snakes mating in a pit while the forest burns around them, and the arms of a dead giant squid rolling limply in the surf. This is what we need to get rid of, what is burning us up, like a warning we did not heed or a wrong we did not right.

The moment Vessel grasps the object the ground begins to shake. Out in the bog orange jets of burning gas flare up and the creaking pumps stop and begin to fall apart in a chorus of slowly bending metal, bangs and clangs. Then we hear the slamming of doors, pounding of steps, and yelling of thick-tongued voices from all around us.

Vessel limps as quickly as he can. We hear shuffling and flapping and panting at every corner, behind every shutter and door, the mud burps and suckles, the tarred wood screams from being scratched by long, thin hands. When I fly higher I see them, a dark crowd filling the streets and alleys like oil seeping from stone. Vessel can't flee into the bog, the tar won't hold his weight and it is said to be bottomless, so he has to stay on the wood.

He struggles along the main thoroughfare, the straightest and shortest passage through the maze of sheds, and almost makes it. But they stream out of the side-streets and alleyways just as he reaches the single road of planks that creeps out into the bog towards land. Vessel faces them with both hands on the smooth, worm-eaten wood of his bladeless oar. The tar people open and flap their stomachs, scrape their bat-fingers, and come at him on the narrow walkway. The sound of wood against claws fills the air, accompanied by the creaking and squeaking and screeching from the collapsing pumps and pipes out on the tar-lake.

During the melee Vessel's left hand suddenly droops from his wrist like a rotten flower and tumbles to the ground. One of the tar people dives forward and catches the limb before it rolls into the bog. As one, Tar's inhabitants rear their pale heads into the air and flutter and smack their gray lips and thick tongues. The tar person throws the loosened body part into the crowd and a meadow of hands rises up to pass it further and further back into the shed maze.

We run. Behind us the dripping torches and smoking jets die down one by one and Tar slowly turns as black as the night.

We crunch across the stone beach to the rowboat, turning occasionally to see if long shadows are following us, but the shore is empty. Vessel launches the rowboat back into the black waves, crawls in and lets the tide carry us slowly away from land.

The horizon is a wound at the edge of the world. Between the red gash and the lid of clouds rises an enormous in-flamed orb that breathes long tongues of conflagration into the void. The heat is like a thousand fires burning.

The closer towards the sun we drift, the hotter the air becomes and the brighter the sky turns. We lie down at the bottom of the rowboat for shade. Vessel's hair fans out on the leaves and he pushes me beneath it for cover, but smoke soon rises from us both and the scent of charred flesh stings our noses.

Vessel cups his hands into the water and soaks us thoroughly. When we start burning again, he cools us with more water. When that is no longer enough, he loosens the branches from his leg and twists the vines that held them in place into a wide loop. He hangs the loop from the stern, takes the carving out of the single pocket of his pants and places it at the bottom of the boat, and slips me gently inside the worn fabric. Then he drops into the water, holding onto the vines with his remaining hand. Thus, we follow the boat further and further out towards the sun.

There is a loud creaking noise and the rowboat shudders as if from an impact. At the bottom of the wood, the carving has swelled up, like a corpse in the ocean. It is now wider than Vessel is tall and still growing. The air itself is screaming and the ocean has started to seethe.

Vessel pulls himself up into the boat, strains against the gigantic stone knot, grunts and groans, and somehow manages to push it over the rim. The carving splashes up a thin spray, before it sinks into the black water. Just a few wide bubbles dissolve on the surface.

But then the water explodes into a plume and something very large and heavy shoots up from the sea. Greasy dark water plunges off it like waterfalls, and a stench so overpowering it makes the smell of the dead giant squid seem like the sweetest perfume, assaults the air. The writhing knot is no longer cold stone, but reeking flesh. It rises and rises, until it reaches the searing sun that just freed itself from the horizon's red grasp.

The twisting rat kings, serpent nests and squid's tentacles envelop the sun like an embrace before dying and slowly start to contract. There is the cry of a million broken-tailed rats, burning vipers, and bursting squid, and the sun disc cracks into a firework of glowing embers that fall from the sky like shooting stars, but are so small they go out before they hit the ocean. Only a sliver of the inflamed sun remains. The heat and light drops to the tepid dusk we have had for almost as far back as I can remember. The remaining pieces of rat, snake and squid plunge into the sea, smelling like singed hair, burned skin and boiled meat. They are so large a flood wave rises from them.

The wave swells and grows and rushes us back to the stony shore much faster than the tide took us out. The flood rolls and churns and reaches far inland, until it is diverted by the rivers and streams and marshes there, and we are finally deposited on dry ground, on a small mound of grass, an abandoned crocodile's nest shaded by vine-choked trees veiled with lichen.

Vessel crawls out of the rowboat and drags himself to the top of the mound, while I lie exhausted on his head. He turns onto his back, places me on his quiet chest and smiles. One by one the stars become visible in the heavens. They are all small and faint and brown, having burned off their white and yellow a long, long time ago.

Among the Living
and the Dead

HE was almost dead. His eyes had sunk into the skull and his nose looked like it had been pinched shut. The skin was ashen and stretched taut over the cheekbones. I couldn't tell how old he was, perhaps my age, or a little younger. There was the hush and chill in the room that always accompanies someone's last hours. But for now he was alive.

As I took my patient in, he drew a hissing breath and shifted slightly in the pillows, but did not open his eyes. I knew how hard that would be in his state. Lifting the eyelids would be like trying to heft a large sack of grain, and the body would be a stone colossus one could never hope to move. I leaned forward to touch his forehead. The white candles on the mahogany nightstand flickered in the draft from my motion and the shadows that hid in the corners of the room trembled and grew. My patient's face was framed by uneven tufts of dark hair, the hairstyle of the sick and dying, cut in bed to reduce warmth and perspiration, yet his skin felt cool and dry and not feverish in the slightest. However, his pulse was barely perceptible and very slow. Had I not seen him move a moment earlier, I might have given up searching for it.

"Lung disease", the request to my recently established practice in Kronstadt had said, but whatever illness held him in its grip had progressed too far for me to stop or even slow it. The only thing I could do was ease physical pain with poppy tincture and even that was risky due to his bad lungs.

A silver rosary with beads of purple glass lay in his lap. As I watched, he shifted again and the rosary started to slide down the sheet. His eyes fluttered. I pulled the rosary up, the chain tinkling.

"Don't worry," I said. "I shall see to it that the rosary remains." He sighed, then grew still. A heavy chair with a back in red brocade stood against the wall. I pulled it across the worn burgundy carpet to the bed and sat down. My patient remained quiet and the room was silent and dark.

I saw the dead: my wife, our children, our parents, siblings, and neighbors. They stroked my cheeks with their hands and spoke soothingly, yet when I woke up I couldn't recall what they or I had said.

Someone was knocking at the door and opening the barrier on its squeaky hinges. I heard myself give a loud snore and opened my eyes, ready to apologize for having dozed off. An elderly woman carrying a tray with a clay jug, a wooden cup, and a plate of bread and cheese inclined her head towards me, then hurried across the floor.

"Here, let me," I said, and reached for the tray.

"Thank you," she said, and smiled, her teeth white and healthy-looking. "One of the cows gave birth last night, so the milk is of the first, and very nourishing. It will strengthen you and your work."

"I think your master may need it more than I do," I said.

"Don't give it to him," she said. "He's too weak. He'll only throw it up and that will sap him even more."

"Don't lose hope yet," I said, although I hadn't seen anyone go this far and return.

"By the way, someone is asking for you," the woman said. "They are waiting in the courtyard."

More patients, I wondered, as I descended the stairs from the bed chamber. Halfway down, a small window illuminated the staircase from a niche in the thick wall. Through the bubble-filled yet colorless glass I could see that the light had turned a bluish gray. My patient had survived the night.

The footman, a middle-aged fellow with dirty-blond hair and square shoulders and large hands, pulled the oak door open. A cold draft rushed towards us, carrying a mist of icy droplets. Outside on the moisture-beaded cobblestones stood a small group of people. Judging from their thick wool jerkins and caps, they were locals. The oldest of them, a small, wiry man, slightly stooped with age, but with a head full of dark, barely-graying hair, approached me. Several of his companions resembled him closely, sons and brothers, I surmised.

"Please leave," the old man said.

I looked at him without hiding my incredulity. "I'm tending to a sick person," I said. "Physicians do not abandon their patients. Besides, he is the master of this domain and your lord."

"That is exactly why we don't want you to help him," the old man said. "We'd be better off without him."

"Why is that?" I said.

"Too many privileges and not enough duties."

"Such as?"

"The right of the first night, for example," the old man said, jutting his chin. "Other lords have abandoned the custom, but our master refuses, saying it's his privilege. There are children,

of course, yet he never acknowledges
them, saying they already have a family.
For every calf or lamb born, our lord
takes just as many as food for himself
and his guests, saying it's his property.
He taxes us freely, yet refuses to send
for a doctor when we need one. But
when he himself is ill . . ."

"That's quite enough," I said. "I
don't care who he is or what he has
done. He's my patient and I will treat
him as best as I can, just as I will any
of you. Are there any sick or injured
that need tending to?"

"Not right now, but there might be
later," the old man said, his mouth a
downward pointing curve.

"Then call for me and I shall as-
sist you freely," I said, ignoring his
threat. "But for now your lord is my
patient."

They muttered and shot me dark
glances, but turned and moved towards the gate. "Why didn't you tell
them we shall lose the master soon

enough?" the old woman asked when I returned inside.

"Let us not assume anything," I said.

The bed chamber held only one window, protected by heavy burgundy drapes. I opened them a little and a stripe of gray light streamed in. I pushed against the old wood to let in some air, but when the frame finally snapped open, the morning was so moist and cold that I shut the window almost immediately. Below I saw part of a thatched roof and a straw-covered, empty pen. A stone parapet surrounded the courtyard, but the corner I could see, from my position, fused with a grassy mound that sloped over the low wall. Beyond the parapet, at the edge of visibility in the fog, I glimpsed the shore of a lake.

My patient seemed to sense that

it was day. He relaxed visibly and his breathing turned less labored. His eyes began moving from side to side beneath their lids, as if he were watching a landscape roll by from a carriage. But the softer drawing of air also made it harder to hear if he was still alive.

I took some bread and cheese and drank from the thin, sweet first milk the matron had brought. As I ate I kept my eyes on my patient in case the sound and smell of food would stir him to waking and hunger. As I had hoped, his eyes stopped moving and his breathing grew faster.

"Have some of this," I said. "It will strengthen you." I held his head up and put the edge of the pitcher to his cracked lips. His throat bobbed eagerly and I poured a little of the liquid into his mouth. He swallowed hard, but shortly thereafter coughed the liquid back up. I turned his head sideways and wiped the milk from his chin and neck with my handkerchief.

"My apologies," I said. "I was hoping you'd manage to keep a little."

His eyes fluttered and I thought I saw a faint nod. I returned to my chair and didn't eat anything more.

As the morning grew into midday and early afternoon, my patient slept several times. I noted his states in my journal, to see if he would make any progress over the next few days. At intervals I opened the window to let in fresh air and ease his breathing. The wind smelled of heather and rain. When it grew dark I closed the drapes and lit the candles on the bedside table. The matron arrived with food. Tonight she had turned the remaining first milk into a pale pudding, served with a few cuts of cured mutton sausage and a jug of yellow water.

"I hope this will be enough, sir," she said. "I'm afraid the larder is rather empty at this time of year, and with the master sick, we haven't been able to procure more."

I handed her a paper note. "Will this buy more food?" I said.

"I will purchase it tomorrow morning," she said, and left me to the meal. I realized I was less hungry than I thought, since I had been sitting still for most of the day, and the sausage cuts and pudding were surprisingly filling. After the meal I warmed the jug with my hands and gave a little water to my patient, but like the previous night he only coughed the fluid back up. It was probably best not to give him anything more that evening.

I was standing at the bottom of the castle walls. They rose out of the ground as if they had been grown instead of built. The dusk was the pale blue of winter. I turned and saw a person standing at the lake a small distance away.

"That must be the lake I saw from the window," I thought. The temperature had sunk further and the ground was sprinkled with snow, the first of the season. But the sound of the wind in the trees and the grass was soft and distant, as if a thick layer of white already covered the land.

I approached the person at the shore. It was a slender man with a proud bearing, eyes ringed by shadows and hair an uneven bristle. He was younger, at least by a decade, than I had assumed from watching him in the chamber. Now a white sheet was draped around his shoulders and trailed along the ground. He began wading into the water, his bare feet leaving no prints on the gray sand.

"Wait!" I said, my breath a mist in the air. He turned towards me, smiled and made a small bow, then continued. Large wet snowflakes alighted on him and the still surface of the lake. The white sheet floated for a moment, like ice, then soaked black and sank.

"Come back!" I said. "Please." But he kept walking until his head vanished beneath the surface.

I woke with a start, the chill from the blue dusk and the slowly falling snow still in my bones. I gazed down at my patient. His eyes were moving fast behind his eyelids, and his breathing was irregular.

In the morning the old man and his relatives were back.

"Is he dead yet?" the elder said.

"How dare you hope for another man's death, no matter how poor a ruler he was?" I said.

"You must leave," the elder said. "This is not your place and you can't stay." His companions turned towards me, their shoulders hunched and their hands balled into fists. "I'm a physician of your lord," I said, hoping my voice wouldn't tremble. "I will leave when he tells me to, not a moment earlier. Now go home."

"Are you prepared to sacrifice everything to save him?" the old man said.

I met his eyes. "Leave," I said. They glared at me, then sauntered towards the gate as if they were guests reluctantly leaving a party, and not intruders being thrown out. When the courtyard was empty, I hurried inside and latched the heavy door.

"Please lower the portcullis," I told the footman.

In the bed chamber I studied my patient's face, searching for hints of arrogance or brutality in the slack-jawed features. Was he really as ruthless a ruler as the old men had described?

In the dream he hadn't seemed cruel, but he wouldn't be the first person to change on his deathbed.

The villagers came again that night, but the portcullis and walls stopped them, as they most probably had other intruders in the past here in the turbulent eastern part of the Habsburg Empire. The unbidden visitors rattled the old iron, banged on the ancient stone, and yelled that they'd give me the same treatment as they would their lord. They didn't leave until dawn grayed the snow-tipped mountains across the valley, and the rooster in the coop in the courtyard started to crow.

My patient was not strong enough to flee. In fact, he seemed a little weaker and had stopped moving altogether. He was so quiet that I had to hold my shaving mirror up to his mouth to see if he was still breathing.

"There must be some way to stop them," I muttered to myself. I knew they would be back, if not that evening, then soon.

"Why are the villagers so eager for their lord to die," I asked the matron when she arrived with hot porridge and honey-sweetened water for breakfast.

"Our master has the power to save everyone, but he refuses to," she said. Tears welled up in her eyes and rolled down her cheeks. She wiped them away with the sleeves of her thick wool jacket.

I thought I knew the answer. I hadn't seen any signs of children or a lady. Presumably the lord had no heirs. If he died, the village would have no formal ruler. It wouldn't be the same as freedom, but it might feel like it for a while.

After the previous night's tension I felt drained and cold, and fell asleep in the chair. Someone touched my shoulder and said:

"You must leave immediately. You are in great danger." His voice was soft, yet clear, without any wheezing.

"I know," I said, too full of sleep to open my eyes. "But I'm not giving you up to the villagers."

"They are not what you should be afraid of."

"Then what is it I ought to fear?" I said.

Suddenly he was close—too close. His breath on my skin was ice cold, like the air from the window. I jerked back, but something sharp stung the side of my neck and bored into it, like Saint Thomas the Incredulous' probing finger. I cried out and woke in the chair by the bed.

The window, whose drapes I had forgotten to close completely, was flickering an ominous red. The stench of smoke filled the room. Outside, bright fire rose in the courtyard.

"I knew I should have put panes on all the roofs after the previous invasion," someone said next to me. My patient was watching me from his bed. He looked pale and weak, but he was awake and speaking.

"Are there horses in the stable?" I said.

He nodded and closed his eyes. "Bridles and saddles are on the wall right by the door."

"You can show me," I said, bundled the sheet around him and lifted him up. He had been sick for so long he was as light as a bird. In the staircase the smoke grew thicker. I stepped inside the alcove and broke the window with a kick, hoping to get some air, but that only made more smoke pour in.

At the bottom of the stairs I pushed hard against the door. I feared it was barred, but it opened easily and noiselessly, and I stumbled into the courtyard. The flagstones were slick with the first snow of the winter. I slid and dropped my patient.

"Are you still alive?" I said, pulling him up and over my shoulder.

"Yes," he whispered, but hung very still.

I carried him across the courtyard and into the stable, which had not caught fire due to its tiled roof. It was almost completely dark, save for the restless, wan light from the flames. I had expected a lot of yelling and screaming, but except for the crackle from the burning wood and the occasional, almost questioning, whinnies from the horses, the courtyard was quiet.

I bridled and saddled the horse closest to the door, lifted my patient up into the seat, then mounted behind him. I took the reins and steered the horse out of the stable, my patient leaning into me, the hooves smashing against the stone.

"Where's the road?" I asked my patient. It probably wouldn't be safe to stay on any public thoroughfare, but I would need to follow it from a distance, as I didn't know the region well enough to find the way back to the city on my own.

"East of the lake," my patient whispered. He slumped and lurched like dead weight, but at least he remained in the saddle. We climbed the small mound I had noticed from the window and crossed the parapet. Beyond it, a long slope led down into the night.

"Hold on," I said. I reined the horse in and started to descend. It was steep and dark and we more slid than rode down to the bottom. When we reached the snow-slick grass I kicked the horse into a gallop. But a musket barked behind us and its ball flew whistling into my back. The horse screamed and reared from the sudden noise, throwing me off. My head struck a rock jutting from the ground, and two of the horse's hooves banged into my chest. I rolled away from the bolting animal, but couldn't get up, my body too heavy.

I coughed, spraying red across my chest. Fluid dripped into my eyes. It was painful to breathe and difficult to see. I hoped the horse and my patient were long gone already, but to my great sadness I saw the horse come trotting out of the gloom. A white figure slid down from the saddle and hobbled close.

Run!" I gasped. "Hurry!" I expected them to be upon us at any moment, once they had gotten down from the castle walls.

"Be still," my patient said above me. His voice seemed far away, and his face was already fading, yet his eyes gleamed brightly in the light from the distant flames. My heart was slowing down, becoming fainter with every throb. How embarrassing to die in front of one's own patient, I thought. What would my teachers and fellow medical students at the University in Vienna have thought if they'd seen this?

My patient's face was very close. His eyes were large and round and he stank of dust and ashes. I shrank away from him. He blinked for a moment, then looked at me as if he just remembered who I was. Then he bowed his head and moved out of view.

"Drink," he said, and put something moist and cool to my lips. I felt very thirsty and swallowed what he offered. It tasted like iron, seared like lye, and spread like arsenic through my body. For a moment it felt like everything had stopped and become very quiet. I was certain I was dead and it was infinitely more peaceful than I had expected. But then sounds began to reach me and the world slid back into view. Strangely, I could move again, as easily and painlessly as before I had been struck from the horse.

"Go, go," my patient hissed, pushing me to my feet. "Run, and don't look back."

"No, I'm not abandoning you," I said.

"It's you they want," he said. "Whatever they told you, it was a ruse to make you stay."

"What?" I said. "Why did they wish me to stay?"

"I can't tell you, I'm sorry, now go!"

"I'm not leaving," I said, and met his eyes. "You are still my patient."

"Go!" he snarled. "Before I kill you myself for breaking my defiance with hunger!" It was as if another face had lain hidden behind his visage, like an iceberg in the ocean. Now it rose to the surface and became fully visible.

His eyes were black and terrible and his teeth were long, gleaming knives. I had heard stories about the living dead, able to heal themselves of any injury or illness, and subsisting on the humors of living beings. Even the grave robbers that procured corpses for the medical students in the capital feared them, but I had always dismissed such stories. Now my certainty was gone.

I scrambled up and away, mounted the horse with my heart pounding in my ears, the taste of blood burning in my mouth, fled across the shivering grass and the hissing heather until I found the road that led out of the village and followed it through the mountain pass and down to the lowland. I turned only once. Through a veil of falling snow I saw him continue, already chest-deep, into the black water of the lake, while the villagers shouted and cried at the shore for him to come back and save them.

Blue Star, Singular Fire

THE blue star glows through a long shaft in the ceiling, as certain celestial bodies did in the burial chambers of the pyramids. We go to sleep, watched over by warm beds and breathing machines. Our eyes and ears and hands reach for that star and move us there, through the quantum veil of time and space, while our tangible selves remain. Since our observations must be corroborated, we are three.

Up close, the star is a burning ocean that billows blue-hot, licking the black void with tongues of white fire. They nip at me, surround and embrace me, threatening to pull me in.

"Come," my companions say, "come."

I turn back to them, slowly, heavily.

Behind us, a tiny, cold world shines, a drop falling through the darkness, ringing like a silver bell. It's not as real or as heavy as the star, yet it captures us like flies in lamp light.

There, in that smaller reality, we are half formed, like dreams, or the fall in temperature when someone steps be-tween you and the sun. Free from our tangible selves, where our attention goes, we go, as quickly as light. To-gether we scour the world for liquids, life and secrets. We begin at the North Pole, then move slowly towards the equator and the southern hemisphere. We are vanguards, forward observers, mapmakers. We know what the others are doing without needing to watch or talk. Our results corroborate.

As we move across the stones and the sand, the scent of coldness rises from a crevice. I reach for it. It may be liquid methane.

"The atmosphere is too thin," they say. "All fluids will have sublimated from the surface. Don't ask us to smell it, like last time."

The finding goes uncorroborated.

When our minds turn weary, we rest, close to the surface. Even inside our repose, corporeally an eternity away, we sleep and dream.

I wake from moving like long, slow waves, giving and being given, accepting and being accepted. It's them, but also me, in unity, in fullness. I sit up and gaze at them in wonder, but they shift and turn away and go on melting together. I move out on the plain, curl up beneath an overhang and try not to be pulled back into them again.

We continue to survey. They stay close together, always in sight of each other. It is not prohibited, it is not allowed, we are free to do what we wish. I lose myself in the planet, in the sand and stone and wind and the lightning that arises when the methane clouds lash the ground. I feel the planet in my hands, eyes, mouth, nose, ears. The planet's core turns warmly, singing as it spins.

"Do you feel it?" I ask them.

"Your results are artifacts instead of facts, and useless," they reply.

I'm about to protest, when the light turns liquid and heat ripples across the sand. Over the mountain-filled horizon the blue star is rising. It was night when we arrived, not day, as I had thought. In this remote dreaming, changes in light and temperature are hard to sense, everything seems the same, disembodied and distant. It requires training and experience to detect. Mine has just failed.

Loops of white flames rear up over the peaks, snapping and tearing at the black ocean around them, like the heads of Hydra, before they fall back down and crash into the seething heliosphere. We flee to the night side of the planet. Here, we sear and burn and scream upon the cold ground. Their hearts flutter in quick, weak waves.

Without a thought of warning they rise and hurl me across the plain. Geysers hiss and spit from the pull of the blue star, magma shakes and roars, threatening to crash through the crust, but we don't notice. I rush back towards them and lash out, throw them against the snow-covered summits in the distance. They reflect the second attack. I evade. We fight in the dunes, in the clouds, on the mountaintops, on the dust devils that roam the plain. We leap and dodge and gasp, trembling with rage and harmful intent. Our shrieks sound like meteors tearing through the atmosphere, like demons in the ancient temple plays. Those plays always end with the protagonists renouncing their former lives, or with death, never anything in between. Now I know why.

But then the blue star catches up with us. Its white fire tongues twist and coil, pull me up and wrap me like a spider in burning silk. It feels like I am sublimating, vanishing, becoming something else. The flames climb far into the universe, slough off what can't keep up with them in enormous blasts, blue-hot, white-burning and gamma-strong.

I don't mean to, but I reach for the two others and fill them with fire from the bright core, from the star, from me. One of them is flung into the purple sky and disappears into the vacuum. Across the peaks, the other screams and appears like a shadow before me, kneeling and clasping their hands in front of them, weeping in sorrow, for mercy. I drip molten blue on the mountains and the plain.

"Go home," I say, "go home."

The shadow turns away and quickly starts to fade. "But what about you?" it says quietly, like a leaf falling through the air, or a whisper of sand across the stone. I don't reply, and then the shadow is gone.

The blue star swallows the bruise-
colored sky whole, magnetic fault
lines shiver and merge in the engulf-
ing, endless light A tiny flicker shoots
up from the planet, becomes caught
in the white tempests that loop out of
the star, and falls back onto the glowing surface with them. The tiny distur-
bance causes small waves to spread on
the seething photosphere, like a pebble
sinking in a pond, before it vanishes
completely.

Apotheosis

BENEATH the smothering, night-dense sky, the line at the fountain of immortality is long, crawling slowly towards the source that shines in the distance. The water has not been tested for pollution or pathogens yet, but people are still eager to drink. The chance that it might confer immortality is enough.

You (or is that I?) wonder how the fountain's water has defeated death. Isn't death, humanity's greatest enemy and obstacle, stronger than that, more difficult to trick? The leveler of empires, of beggars, and kings, defused by a simple drink? But in a scream, a shock, a stab of insight, you realize: The fountain doesn't grant immortality, but death. The only way to become immortal is to embrace death completely and die then and there. You rush up and shout this information to the others in line, but before you can even finish the sentence, several people give in to the source and die. The others back away from the water, now seeing the full price of its gift.

"I knew it was too good to be true," one of them mutters and leaves.

"Me too. I never win anything, ever," another says and shuffles quietly away.

Dejected, the crowd dissolves and starts on the long way home, through the forests, across the mountains, past the marshes, back to the towns and suburbs and cities, with the hopes of attaining what humanity desires the most, crushed, like fake diamonds beneath glass.

But now you have been noticed, singled out, like the gaze of a stranger, of someone who doesn't know you yet, but really wants to. You sense it and deny it and hope it means nothing.

You (or is that I?) return home to the concrete canyons and glass valleys, to another place, another crowd, this time at the cinema, accompanied by a female friend. In the red and gold velvet hall, the lights go out, the curtains draw aside, and the 16:9 face of the celluloid screen awakens. From the audience you watch the film together with your friend. In retrospect you can't say how it was or what it was about, only that in the intermission you and your friend flow out into the foyer with the rest of the crowd and sit down at a small, round table. There you enjoy a sugary latte and salted peanuts, before you return, ready to watch the second half of the feature.

But beneath the shadow puppet theater emitted by the film projector, the screen is always blank and smooth and bright, despite what goes on in the movie, what the characters say or do, whether they are happy or sad or lonely or connected, no matter how large their houses are or how many children they get. Everyone sees that blankness of the movie, all the time, yet do not notice it because they are so used to watching the shadows instead of the source of the light. But now you sense it and see it, and because of that, you become vulnerable to it.

Thus, people in the audience begin to die, consumed by the end that would have waited for them for the rest of their natural lives, no matter how long it would have taken, like a faithful lover. Now it has been released from its temporal bonds and rushes towards them, like the future, reaches for them across the months and years and decades to merge in the now. One person has a heart attack, another chokes on their own tongue, a third strokes out. Everyone who are still able to start screaming, not only because the person next to them has died in a sudden and spectacular way, but because they can feel their own death pulling at them as well, beckoning them in the same direction as the already departed. But once the audience gets to its feet and starts emptying the theater, the moment is over and the dying is almost done.

You (or is that I?) turn to look at your friend for reassurance, but she perishes, with bulging eyes and gaping mouth. You are death and death is you! Infested now with what you denied at the source past the mountains and the forests and the marshes, you have become it yourself. The realization rings in your mind, your heart, your gut. You take in the people around you, but say nothing, warn them not, because they won't believe you, have no way to understand. They start to singe and curl at the edges, like celluloid on fire. You shift your gaze and death moves with it, but not to every person you look at, just one and two here and there, so that no one can feel safe.

"I am death!" you (or is that I?) scream silently, from the ecstasy of true immortality, from death, your own as well as that of others. Then you stand and wade into the crowd.

Summer Dusk,
Winter Moon

WE SPENT twelve harvests of
barley, six of wheat, three of
potatoes, one of turnip, the milk from
a hundred cows, the meat from fifty
pigs, twenty oxen, ten chicken, two
whales, three yearly catches of cod, one
of salmon, one of eel, the pink bind-
weed flowers from an entire meadow
of long-bladed grass strangled by their
vines, half a field of black poppies, a
garden of purple violets, ten crops of
cotton, five of linen, the wool from
six hundred sheep, the furs from three
hundred mountain stoats, and nine

thousand liters of fresh, clean water. For every year he had been gone, the amount of resources needed to call him back increased sharply, like the outline of a mountain. That is how we awoke Summer Dusk from death.

In the stone casket under the wide colonnade in the mausoleum made of black marble veined with gold at the end of the long icy hallway, Summer Dusk's time reversed, turning his body from a dried-up corpse to a living, breathing person. His shriveled flesh bulged, then relaxed, infused with life anew, the cheekbones and eye sockets filled out, his skin softened and gained color, warm fluid began running through his blood vessels again, its touch enlivening everything like the sun in spring. Finally, Summer Dusk's chest moved in a sudden inhalation. Slowly, he opened his eyes and sat up and took in the faces of his family and relatives, mentors and friends, ministers and parliament members, as if roused from a long, but pleasant sleep. When he recognized us, he smiled and reached for us, like a child.

But death yields nothing without resistance and caught hold of Summer Dusk with long and hungry fingers. His golden eyes went black with fear, dark rivers blossomed in his narrow face, and his long, lithe body, as much female as male, shriveled and softened and withered again in a tug of war between our granted life and death's lonely selfishness. We should perhaps have let him go then, but there was no way we could do that. Instead, we gasped and put our hands to our mouths and dared barely watch.

Finally, Summer Dusk's features turned ashen, his nails and lips darkened to purple as if he were very, very cold, and black bled into his sky-blue hair. His lilac filigree armor, which we had buried him in so he would always be ready to fight, tarnished to the color of night. His slim golden sword, which we had left in his right hand so he would always be able to defend us, melted and the liquid metal sank into the black marble. He looked dead, yet still he gazed at us with an expression of utter terror and took us in, one by one, as if he begged us to release him. Summer Dusk was no longer dead, but not wholly alive either. As we slowly realized what had happened, a terrible silence fell in the room. Many of his relatives started weeping, but without a sound.

"Please forgive us, beloved hero!" Summer Dusk's favorite member of parliament said, with much hand-wringing. "A terrible foe has entered the land and now we implore you, who defeated the stone birds of Aa, the fire waves in Ghoresh, the ice forest at Lath, and the water labyrinth on Velled, to come to our aid once again."

It was a familiar call, one we had used many times before, and which, at more occasions than we cared to count, Summer Dusk had answered, always with a soft smile and crinkled eyes. But now he simply rose from his cold bedding, without a word, without looking at us. He closed his gauntlet-sheathed hands around the bled-out remains of his sword and wrenched it out of the black marble, the blade now a jagged narrow length of stone. The cloak of soft ermine fur that we had draped around his shoulders for warmth and comfort slid to the floor. Then Summer Dusk left the mausoleum, a layer of frost on every surface.

None dared step between Summer Dusk and whatever goal he had in mind. To our relief he left the capital, then traveled north to the region where the crops that had been used to awaken him were grown, the most fertile area in the realm. There he knelt in a stubbly field and all around him black saplings poked like claws out of the cold earth. The saplings grew and grasped at one another while they reached for the sky like hungry beasts and grew into a tall black forest with twisted trunks and leafless branches. For one day's journey around the forest the land turned to marsh and the water that bled from it was black and dank. Here, gales blew constantly, the rain lashed sideways, and it was always dark. The farmers and woodcutters who didn't flee the region turned quiet and listless and their crops drowned in the mud.

Since Summer Dusk's sky blue hair, golden eyes, and lilac armor had turned as black and glistening as the snow-gleaming nights before December solstice, we renamed him Winter Moon. We sent envoys and messengers to parlay with him, but they could not find their way through the lightless forest. We sent hunters and scouts, but they could not find him in the pathless wood. We sent navigators and explorers, and they followed the direction that the trees and branches hunched and all fluid seeped away from, no matter the elevation, to the middle of the forest. There they found Winter Moon kneeling in a clearing covered by grass as sharp and dark as obsidian. The explorers and navigators slung the warm ermine cloak around his shoulders, conveyed our sincerest apologies and begged him to save us, their breath white upon the icy air, but he remained still and silent. We sent poets and bards with the navigators and explorers to fully express how much we loved him and needed him, but he stayed immobile and quiet.

In our towns and cities, the printing presses roared and shook, and spat out stack upon stack of journals and magazines that were brought to crowded squares and busy street corners, debating whether Winter Moon was still a friend or had become a foe since he didn't want to help us and what might happen if we failed to awaken his compassion. We had exhausted all our other heroes.

In the mean time, the amorphous mass of spine-covered tendrils and gnashing mouths that had eaten all the cod and halibut and herring and crabs and sea urchins and mussels along our southern coast and sent the fishermen and shellfish divers in five regions into starvation, necessitating aid in the form of flour and grain from the capital, had crawled up on land and started to consume the fields and forests and everything that lived there, leaving nothing but a glistening slug-trail in its wake. And while doing so, the monster grew in size and hunger. The local authorities reported that the terror was on its way inland and that during its slimy journey the monster had gained a taste for meat, because now it moved directly towards meadows with livestock, instead of the fields of crops and copses of trees it had previously aimed at.

At first we tried to direct the horror with straw lures of cows and sheep dressed in hide or fur from the appropriate species, but the monster didn't always crawl in that direction. Then we made cow and sheep-shaped sculptures from meat that was off or otherwise unfit for human consumption, and our control of the horror's wanderings became more accurate. Best of all worked live animals, which made the monster go exactly where we desired, but with the fish and crops in several regions gone, we could only afford to use real livestock to lead the monster away from the largest villages and towns. However, that worked just for a limited amount of time. As the terror gained in size, it also seemed to become hungrier and more determined. A few cows and sheep were no longer enough to tempt it away from population centers. Instead, the monster began following paths and roads to the next town or village.

We reported all of this to Winter Moon via navigator-emissaries that read clippings from the most recently printed magazines and journals aloud to him, but he remained quiet and immobile.

We sent fusiliers and cavaliers, but the horror from the sea just swallowed them up, spat the metal parts out, and swelled further in girth. We sent grenadiers and cannoneers, but they merely slowed the terror. Now the monster seemed to go directly for soft and easily digested human flesh, instead of fur-covered and thick-skinned livestock. We made more lures, this time sculptures shaped like humans made from animal flesh. Again it worked for a little time, until the terror consumed a scientist's apprentice that ventured too close and a coach of tourists on their way to the capital, and stopped turning toward the flesh statues. Still Winter Moon did nothing.

We needed help and quickly. It was then we had a bright and awful idea. We sent the destitute and addicted from the capital, by offering help to their dependents if they were willing to make the journey. When they ran out, we transferred the fishermen and shellfish divers that had fled inland to seek new jobs. Lastly, we ordered the local farmers and villagers that had lost their fields and meadows to the monster. Experiments with various formations and patterns showed that dense clusters of people were not necessary to move the horror in the desired direction. It wasn't even pertinent for the bodies to stand close together. Instead, a long, thin row of soft and easily digested flesh was enough. In open areas the lures could be spread out with a distance of up to ten meters, like a line of breadcrumbs snaking to the witch's house. But in places with denser vegetation and reduced visibility, such as in Winter Moon's forest, they had to be positioned closer together.

Finally the horror arrived, closed its gelatinous mass around the twisted trunks and leafless branches, and subsumed them into itself with a terrible snapping and creaking and cracking. Slowly, the monster ate its way through the dark forest, to the black heart where Winter Moon knelt upon the obsidian grass, the ermine cloak still around his shoulders, but the fur now grey from sleet and mud. We

prayed that when the terror discovered
Winter Moon it would try to eat him.
Then Winter Moon would be forced
to defend himself, and by extension,
us. The moment rushed close, the horror was almost upon Winter Moon,
taller than the cruel trees and wider
than the clearing in which he sat. Now,
now, nearer and nearer, soon our hero
would leap into action as he had done
so many times in the past. Closer and
closer, until the monster blotted out
our view of Winter Moon completely,
and we couldn't see what went on behind its trembling bulk. Our journalists and scientists stretched their necks
and stood on their toes. Who would
have the honor of first sending their
report about Winter Moon's reawak-
ened heroism to their editor or supe-
rior? Beyond the line of scientists and
journalists, the rest of us waited. But
the terror from the sea simply slid past
Winter Moon, so close that the sticky
edges of its slimy trail lapped against

Winter Moon's tarnished greaves and glued the hairs on the hem of his ermine cloak together.

But now the monster had caught the scent of large amounts of human flesh. It stopped and reared up and sampled the air with its innumerable mouths and pale tongues, shivering in expectation. It was just three days' travel away from the capital. Now the horror turned in that direction, with renewed purpose and speed. Frantically, we pooled all we had left of meat and fur and leather, but now nothing could tempt the horror away from our densest population center. We sounded the alert to evacuate the capital, and started transporting the merchants and craftsmen and soldiers and academics and government officials and ministers in overfilled coaches and people-spilling barges in the opposite direction of the monster from the sea.

A short distance from the city, right before Capital Road turns away from the ocean and reaches inland, there is a narrow but deep canyon. That crevice is a scar from the attacks of the last monster Winter Moon defeated, but whose venom killed him in the end. Here, fresh water fell like veils from the steep edges of the chasm down to a large transparent pool as cold and pure as the eternal snow in the north. Vines of fragrant purple honeysuckle draped the stone walls and filled the air with their perfume. Slowly, the horror began seeping into the canyon to consume the liquid and vegetation in its heart. At that moment Winter Moon's all-black eyes flew open and he started running.

The journalists and scientists that trailed the monster later reported that as it reached the inner aromatic corner of the canyon and started draining the icy water, something bright shot up over the mass of lapping, smacking mouths and a keening noise sliced through the air. Winter Moon's tarnished armor gleamed dully in the faint light from the stars and with his black sword raised like the gate to the underworld he pierced the horror. The mouths shrieked and wailed and the tendrils lashed at their assailant with long sharp spines.

※

There, in the subterranean darkness, among the falling water and the fragrant flowers, Winter Moon fought the monster for five days and five nights. He cut and sliced and severed each sharp and whipping tendril, but for each one he hacked off, three new arose. The monster shook and roared and attacked. On the sixth day Winter Moon was hunched and staggering, with gashes and lacerations scarring his armor. His black blood dripped down on the horrid mass and the thousand mouths lapped it up while they moaned and groaned in endless hunger. But where Winter Moon's blood fell, the gelatinous mass stopped moving and became as hard and still as stone. Winter Moon glanced down at the petrified flesh and fought with renewed vigor.

Finally, he had cut his way into the center of the shivering, reeking blob. Here, instead of mouths, the monster had a multitude of entirely too human-looking blue, green, gray and brown eyes that rolled and glared as if they were bringing down a thousand curses upon Winter Moon. But also they turned to stone when he bled upon them. Winter Moon stopped and stood for a moment, swaying slightly in the star-pierced gloom. Then he threw his black sword away. It spun and glittered through the air, hit the surface of the pool en pointe, and shattered into a thousand pieces, before it sank into the cold depths. Dense clusters of spine-covered tendrils shot up and coiled around Winter Moon's wrists and ankles. He bucked and thrashed like a salmon in a bear's grip, but the tendrils embraced his chest and head and bent him slowly backwards, exposing his throat. Some of us realized what would happen next and averted our gaze in respect, others could not turn away from the spectacle. The glaring eyes and gnashing mouths passed the sharp spine of a tendril across the ashen skin, unhurriedly and lazily, almost like an afterthought. Winter Moon stiffened like the oracles that shiver and shake in the temples, but made no sound. At first nothing happened, but then a black crescent grew across his pale throat, a few drops seeping out from the gash. Then the dam broke and a spray of cold blood spurted high and rained down on the trembling mass.

Before our eyes the horror turned to stone. The mineral spread quicker than pox, transforming the fetid flesh to hard, gray granite. Sharp fissures gouged through the mineral until the entire monster cracked like an egg, and fell down on the golden shore in the heart of the canyon.

We picked Winter Moon up from the stinking, slime-covered shards and brought him home to the mausoleum made of black marble veined with gold at the end of the long icy hallway. His head was almost severed from his neck, but we stitched it back on with our thinnest needles and our finest silk thread, and when we were done the seam was hardly visible at all. We washed Winter Moon's face and armor with honeysuckle-scented water, combed and anointed his hair, and pulled a cloak of shiny black ermine fur around his shoulders. We lowered him into a coffin made from crystal, which allowed us to see him, yet blurred the cuts in his face and armor. All his family and relatives, mentors and friends, ministers and parliament members were present. Then we pushed the transparent lid into place and stepped back to take our hero in and the tears that rolled down our cheeks were as crimson as the dusk in summer. That is how we buried Winter Moon the second time.

www.ingramcontent.com/pod-product-compliance
Lightning Source LLC
Chambersburg PA
CBHW032040180726

48284CB00008B/2670